READING CORNER

My Nan

A humorous
rhyming story

First published in 2006 by
Franklin Watts
338 Euston Road
London
NW1 3BH

Franklin Watts Australia
Hachette Children's Books
Level 17/207 Kent Street
Sydney
NSW 2000

A CIP catalogue record for this book is available
from the British Library.

ISBN 0 7496 6547 5 (hbk)
ISBN 0 7496 6554 8 (pbk)

Series Editor: Jackie Hamley
Series Advisors: Dr Barrie Wade, Dr Hilary Minns
Design: Peter Scoulding

Printed in China

My Nan

Written by
Jillian Powell

Illustrated by
Maddy McClellan

W
FRANKLIN WATTS
LONDON•SYDNEY

Jillian Powell

"My nana had auburn hair and wore earrings like blackberries. I can still remember jumping up with excitement when she came to visit."

Maddy McClellan

"My nan lived on the other side of the world so I hardly ever got to see her. The only thing I really remember is that she liked marzipan covered in chocolate!"

My nan is not like other nans.

She eats hot dogs and drinks from cans.

She does things that annoy my mum –

– like blowing bright-pink bubble gum.

7

While other nans knit
socks and jumpers,
my nan likes to
drive big dumpers.

Some nans dress up in gloves and suits. Mine wears hard hats and welly boots.

Other nans have dogs or cats,
but my nan has fifteen pet rats!

Some nans teach budgies how to talk –
mine takes her rats out for a walk.

11

Most nans like gentle sports like bowls.

My nan is out there scoring goals.

When you're at your nan's for tea,

do you have such fun as me?

Your nan can surely bake a cake,
but mine knows how to charm
a snake.

Some nans go to evening classes,
catch the bus with cheap bus passes.

But my nan says

the bus is slow.

Her motorbike can really go!

When your nan takes you to the park,
she gets you home before it's dark.

She helps you reach the monkey rings
and doesn't stay out on the swings.

Some nans have hobbies like
brass-rubbing.

But my nan likes to go out clubbing.

She loves the music really loud,
and lets her hair down in a crowd.

23

When other nans sit down to rest,
mine goes to take her flying test.

24

She loops the loop and spins around
while we stand watching from the
ground.

Your nan may give you simple treats like lollipops and bags of sweets.

She takes you shopping in the sales, while mine takes me out watching whales!

While other nans are watching soaps,
my nan is learning to climb ropes.

Some nans have problems
with their knees,
but my nan swings
from a trapeze.

No other nans are like my nan –
they can't do half the things she can.
But I would never swap my nan,
because ...

... I am her biggest fan!

Notes for parents and teachers

READING CORNER has been structured to provide maximum support for new readers. The stories may be used by adults for sharing with young children. Primarily, however, the stories are designed for newly independent readers, whether they are reading these books in bed at night, or in the reading corner at school or in the library.

Starting to read alone can be a daunting prospect. READING CORNER helps by providing visual support and repeating words and phrases, while making reading enjoyable. These books will develop confidence in the new reader, and encourage a love of reading that will last a lifetime!

If you are reading this book with a child, here are a few tips:

1. Make reading fun! Choose a time to read when you and the child are relaxed and have time to share the story.

2. Encourage children to reread the story, and to retell the story in their own words, using the illustrations to remind them what has happened.

3. Give praise! Remember that small mistakes need not always be corrected.

READING CORNER covers three grades of early reading ability, with three levels at each grade. Each level has a certain number of words per story, indicated by the number of bars on the spine of the book, to allow you to choose the right book for a young reader:

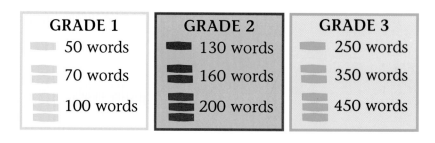

GRADE 1	GRADE 2	GRADE 3
50 words	130 words	250 words
70 words	160 words	350 words
100 words	200 words	450 words

100
LITTLE POEMS

BY

MARGARET SACKVILLE

EDINBURGH: THE PORPOISE PRESS

1928

℃ First published in 1928
by The Porpoise Press
133A George Street
Edinburgh, C.

℃ Of this edition fifty
copies have been printed
on Arches French hand-
made paper, consecu-
tively numbered, and
signed by the Author,
and bound in full cloth.

821
1044

℃ Printed in Great Britain by
The Riverside Press Ltd.
Edinburgh, Scotland

CONTENTS

5

¶ Many of these poems have already appeared in different collections under the heading *Epitaphs*, but are here given a somewhat wider application. For permission to reprint certain of these, acknowledgment is made to Messrs George Allen & Unwin, Ltd.

6

DEDICATION

To R. C. M.

You have always looked kindly on these verses, and encouraged me to add to their number. So there is no one to whom I can dedicate them more fittingly than to you. But the mood which inspired them has already dissolved, and I cannot help feeling that they express a sort of detached melancholy which curiously misrepresents my *permanent* attitude towards life.

You will notice what may be described as a change of temperature in the more recent productions. I am not a pessimist, as you know!

THINK not that verse
Which, like the wind,
Blows, wailing, from
The poet's brain,

Proves him perverse
Towards his kind,
Deliberately
In search of pain.

Laughter he loves
Like any child,
And as a boy's
His heart is gay;

Only he moves
As one exiled
From kingdoms long since
Passed away.

And ancient memories,
Deep-stored
In the recesses
Of his heart,

The magic frees
Of some chance word,
And then a veil
Is rent apart.

So lives he, haunted
By old grief
And passions he
Has never known,

But which, translated,
Bring relief
To ghostly sorrows
Not his own.

JOY

I KNEW Joy once and, after, could not bear
That any lesser joy should follow her;
So died. How else escape the thing men call
Delight?—Poor men who know her not at all!

SONGLESS SLEEP

THE scent of faded roses, once a-bloom,
Bring; but no living roses to my tomb:
Nor any song. Through songless Summer hours
I waked—then slept with Summer and her flowers.

TRIUMPH

MY Day has dawned and loud within my ears
    I hear, exultant as a roaring sea,
That cry my kinsman uttered at Poitiers,
    Upon the Field in France—*Jour de ma Vie!*

SIX PORTRAITS

I

Neither of Earth nor Heaven, here she lies,
Poor troubled ashes, gentle and unwise.

II

I mastered Life and did bestride him well.
But Death's another matter. Here I fell.

III

Lonely I lived and died. Let no foot-fall
Disturb me now—for that were worse than all!

IV

I gambled high with Life. The game is done;
But who shall say if I have lost or won?

V

Patient and bent, he trod a stony road—
A little body under a great load.

VI

Earth, air, fire, water made me. Each in turn
Caused me to soar and stumble, freeze and burn.

OBLIVION

As some great house of noble stone
Is wrecked and broken in upon,
Break up my words and deeds. Let none
Know where I've stood or whither gone.

BEAUTY

My beauty was so fine and rare
You'd think it woven out of air;
Like a web of wind and sun.
How like a breath of air 'tis gone!

AT ASSOUAN

Tread softly, O, my dancing feet!
Lest your untimely gladness stir
Dust of forgotten men, who find death sweet,
At rest within their sepulchre.

SUMMER LIFE

A handful of wild thyme—a breath, a song.
This was my life. I lived a Summer long;
Lived, loved and died. To love a Summer through
And then to die! What better could I do?

I DIED so long ago
    That none may tell
My name, my place, my labour or my fame:
    Thus I sleep well.

PRIDE

EXILED am I, yet still with unbowed head
Accept my pittance—water and dry bread;
More royal in my poverty and proud
Than kings who from their thrones placate the crowd.

EVERYMAN

WHAT shall be said of me? "He lived a span—
Then died." No more! What more of any man?

A SIGH

A SAD wind lifts and stirs
    The fallen leaves;
My life was short as theirs,
    Yet no wind grieves!

FOR A BABE

Too soon
I rose
Before
The sun
Was hot;
The waning moon
Saw me, at the night's close,
Enter ere day'd begun
My grassy cot.

THE ACCIDENT

BECAUSE too proud almost to live or die
I walked, despising earth, ambitiously,
Earth took revenge; for I, when all seemed well,
Over this mound of earth stumbled and fell.

TREACHERY

A soft breeze slew me. Many a blind gale
Beat with both hands upon my tattered sail
Vainly. So death, who lay in wait for me,
Drowned me in harbour in a Summer sea.

JOY

Joy, perch above my sleeping head
And I shall know I am not dead.

Oh, shed your song in drops of sound,
Piercing this hard and grudging ground

With golden drops of shining song;
So my brief night shall not seem long.

RELEASE

For long my feet were captive things;
Now I have changed my feet for wings.

FOAM

My life is finished which was all delight:
Now the moon rises. Scatter upon me
A handful of salt-water, cold and bright;
Rainbows of foam and bubbles of the sea.

Now her golden self is gone,
Cut her image in white stone,
And in deep wood let her lie
Under tangled greenery;
Hidden in a quiet shrine,
Where, all night, a lamp shall shine,
That travellers who pass this way
Here entering may rest till day.
Let books, flowers, pictures, grace
Her retired dwelling-place,
So her carven beauty shall,
Still unconquered, hold men thrall,
And her lovers counted be
On, throughout eternity.
Loyal suitors here shall press
Round her cloistered loveliness,
Where, through softest sleep, she gives
Such radiance forth, and, dead, yet lives.

FOR A BLIND MAN

On many a road, forlorn,
    I wandered day and night.
For *this* then was I born—
    To find in death my light?

CONSUMMATION

I'll lay me down without a word:
The deepest prayer is still unheard;
And only silence may express
This last and perfect loneliness.

THE HANDICAP

Like Icarus, I flew
    To scale the starry way,
But wings might nothing do
    Against my feet of clay.

A PAUSE

ALL's done,
All's said;
To-night
In a strange bed
Alone
I
Lie,
So slight,
So hid,
As in
A chrysalid
A butterfly.

THE DUNCE

ALAS, this rhyme!
    Ill-spelt, ill-writ,
I had no time
    To copy it;

So read no more
    But say that night
Gripped me before
    I'd learnt to write.

BONNE-NUIT

(FOR A CHILD)

FROM hedge and copse
    The glow-worms peep,
Each wild rose drops
    Its head in sleep.
Done is my day
    Of sun and light,
I'll cease from play
    And say " Good-night."

18

THIRST

LIFE did not stint my cup to fill,
I drank each drop yet thirsted still;
Death's little, poor and meagre wine
Has wholly quenched this thirst of mine.

HAPPY SLEEP

THOUGH life was good
  I find sleep best:
Even happy things
  Have need of rest.

MEMORIAL

LEAVE me alone,
  O, Friend! This unmarked place
Better befits than stone
  My burial place.

Your thought of me
  May it be light as fallen leaves, and let,
Rather than such obtruded memory,
  All men forget.

DREAM FULFILLED

I DREAMED. The dream came true. A lightning stroke
Stabbed me awake. I perished as I woke.

A HEART

If one should take into his hand
A little shining heap of sand,
Open, and let it sea-ward fly—
That was my heart and such am I.

POET'S TOMB

Commend me not : you praise
   A thing unknown,
Nor mark my scattered days
   With pomp of stone ;
Neither condemn : I was
   Through all my time
Obedient to the laws
   Of vagrant rhyme.

THE FALSE MISTRESS

I had a name, a place, who now have none,
For all I was lies crushed beneath a stone.
Fame was my Mistress, but a crumbling name
On a grey stone is all I've had of Fame !

ANOTHER PORTRAIT

His life was like white steel—a mind
Keen as the wind, yet ever kind.
Like an eager wind he blew
Through the world. He loved a few,
Hated none. Beneath his wings
Crowds of little, helpless things
Found shelter. These shall surely keep
Trusty watch about his sleep.

GREEN FRUIT

O! ROSE-RED blossom, shake your wings and fall
From the safe shelter of the sunny wall!
Your fruit? Lament it not. It might have been
Like mine (which came to ripeness), sour and green.

THE MEETING PLACE

"*I* WANDERED over seas." "From one green glade
Not once *my* unadventurous footsteps strayed."
"Each road on earth in turn received *my* feet."
"We might have never met." "Yet here we meet!"

THE AMBUSH

YEAR out, year in, I took my daily pleasure
In ways serene beyond the common measure,
So was the more surprised when, suddenly,
Death (whom I scarce believed in) sprang on me.

JOURNEY'S END

My wandering feet at last have found
Peace in a little space of ground;
My feet, which ever scorned to rest,
Here mark the end of every quest.

THE CONFIDANT

BREAK not my silence, trouble not my sleep;
A weighty secret's given me to keep!
Life's confidant was I, but what he said
None knows, nor what Death tells me now I'm dead.

My Burial Place
Let no man mark ;
Grant me this grace—
    Unbroken sleep,
    Serene and deep
Through the warm dark.

THE HONOUR

HUMBLY I lived but very proudly died,
Death's chosen ! Can you wonder at my pride?—
Philosophers and Heroes, Saints and Kings
He left—but folded *me* beneath his wings.

THE WATCHER

By angry breakers caught and overcome,
I sank, as sinks a vessel through the foam ;
And now incurious and calm I lie,
Watching the keels of other ships go by.

A LITTLE wind,
Eager and shrill,
Has blown my withered
Years away;

You shall not find,
Search where you will,
One of those withered
Years to-day.

THE CHALLENGE

LIFE, like a glove,
I here fling down
And claim (so long denied!)
Renown.

Well content
My all to give,
That, being dead,
My fame may live.

THE UNKNOWN FRIEND

KINDER than life, this sudden, soft surprise
Falling, like longed-for sleep on waking eyes !
If *this* be death that men so much defame,
Let death—let life—take each the other's name !

THE RETURN

DISOWN me not, O ! patient Mother Earth !
Restless was I—a rebel from my birth ;
But now thy prodigal and weary son
Seeks pardon at thy breast, his folly done.

THE OUTCAST

THIS flickering light, these silences and showers
   Were loved by me—yea, more than my own kind :—
So give these last grey ashes, frail as flowers,
   To the chill comfort of a passing wind.

LONELY SLEEP

I WOKE and called aloud but none replied ;
   My bed was lonely and the night was deep ;
So, growing tired, I turned upon my side,
   Dozed for an hour or two—then went to sleep.

TIME'S REVENGES

How many generations yet shall pass
Ere these poor ashes blossom into grass,
What stars be quenched, what million years unclose,
Before I shake forth perfume like a rose?

PROPHECY

My light is out, yet will I prophesy
Men still unborn will show more light than I;
And am content that other men in turn
Against *my* darkness shall the brighter burn.

SECURITY

THE myriad roots of the entwining grass
Have shut me in from all that once I was.
Nor may a thought, however subtle, break
Through this green roof. Speak loud! I shall not wake.

THE SLAYERS

"WHY did you die?"—I died of everything:
    Life, like deep water, robbed me of my breath;
Sorrow, delight, love, music, Winter, Spring
    Slew me in turn, and, last of all, came—Death.

THE SUMMONS

Early and late, I, listening heard
Time sweeping by without a word,
Till with a silent gesture, he
Called *me* to share his secrecy.

THE DREAMER

Oh, why disturb me where I'm lying,
Small birds of Spring, with your shrill crying?
Leave me in peace, for dreams are bringing
Me sharper joy than all your singing.

SEA-WRACK

My flesh was water and my spirit foam;
Storm was my peace; the changing tides my home.
But now on these swift tides I drift no more,
Cast up like weed upon an unknown shore.

NIGHT-FALL

Night falls and patient still
 I wait, nor know at all
What unknown fears may fill
 The lonely interval.

Or if to harbour caught,
 From these impatient seas,
I find my lost, long-sought,
 Golden Hesperides !

PROUD BEAUTY

Nothing remains :
 No perfume clings
Of all these rains
 And all these Springs.

Nor of that beauty
 Which none knew
To wear as well
 As I could do.

All past, all done with :
 Scented rain,
Song, beauty, Spring—
 And my disdain.

FINALE

THIS quiet pillow
  Share with me,
Till time also
  Has ceased to be.

Time, whose rough hand
  Has harshly spread
Our little, poor and
  Narrow bed

To serve his stern
  And tedious whim—
Yet we in turn
  Shall bury him!

VALE

EYES, heart and brain,
  Here shall forget
The sun and rain.

Wild grasses, wet
Leaves soaked in dew,
  Let such regret

With choicer tears,
And rarer grief
Than ours, a thing so brief
  It lived its span of years
And still was new!

FAME

THE laurel crown
 Above my head
Has fallen down,
 Its leaves are dead :

And no one ever
 Comes this way,
Even to sweep
 The leaves away.

THE BANKRUPT

THAT still unpunished cheat,
 To-morrow (now To-day)
Pays so much in the pound
Then goes his way.

TIME

MAGICIAN Time,
 What secret thing
Lies underneath
 Your silent wing?

No stranger portent
 Or surprise
Than *this* year seen
 With *last* year's eyes!

ON WOMAN

DECEPTIVE Woman ! When all's said and done
Your wit lies often in your face alone,
And simple man is still amazed to find
Singular beauty cloak a common mind.

CONTENT

THESE quiet days have wrapped my senses round
In softest silence, perfumed and profound ;
Wrapped in a golden web of night and noon,
Content I lie—a moth in a cocoon.

ARROGANCE

THESE pinnacles of Thought
    Which sought to scale the sky
Are down, like Babels brought,
    And all in ruins lie.

And towers which should have flown
    Have tumbled to one side,
Because their wings were stone—
    O! vast and vanquished pride.

PRISONERS

O, EAGER thoughts ! Too fleet
  To serve this lagging brain,
What are you?—Birds which beat
  Against a window-pane?

A COUNSEL

O, CAREFUL mind ! If joy be but a dream,
  No less is grief. Oh, better far to be
Duped by the sun's reflection in a stream
Than by this dull deceit of misery.

THE STRANGER

A LITTLE Joy,
So light of wing,
Perched on my window-sill
To-day.

I knew a lovelier
Joy last Spring.
And drove that stranger
Joy away.

A WARNING

O, SINGER ! Fear that melancholy wind
Which blows from some lost region of the mind,
Lest thy high courage shudder to despair
As flying men are shipwrecked in mid-air.

INVOCATION

O, SUMMER, Summer, grant me words to greet
The resurrection of thy passing feet !
Alas ! Thy suns have set me out of tune,
As birds are silenced of their songs in June.

EDEN REVISITED

Is this remembered Paradise ? Alas !
  How changed and drifted from its former state !
" No man may find lost Eden as it was :
  Pass on ! " replied the Guardian of the Gate.

BEAMS

In secret, out of sight,
   My days like petals fall,
Or dancing beams of light
   Which make no sound at all.

A SONG

Song is a mirror where Love's face,
   Radiant yet cool, reflected lies;
So clouds have caught the sun's red blaze
   And filled with harmless fire the skies;

So shot with flame cold waters run,
   Bright, frozen, passionless and free,
Bearing unscathed a phantom sun
   In mimic ardour, towards the sea.

OUT OF STRENGTH SWEETNESS

How from this cold, deliberate thought
   Might such impetuous beauty spring?
And who Athene's owl has taught,
   Like careless birds, to preen and sing?

Thus, long ago, Pygmalion,
   Who with unflagging will had striven,
Called forth a living maid from stone
   And so accomplished earth and heaven.

Not with the fallen flesh
 Shall Beauty fade,
But rather bloom afresh,
 Re-born, re-made,
Turning her flame within
 That all may see
Shine, through the wrinkled skin,
 Her dignity.

ANOTHER SONG

Linger no more,
 Upon the brink
  Of Song;
Plunge boldly, or
 These swelling tides will shrink
  To sand ere long.

Oh! claim her now,
 Thy joy unproved
  Fly on!
Remember how
 Cold Artemis with lofty passion loved
  Endymion.

Plunge, soar, but still
 Thy wingèd bliss
  Pursue;
Pause not until,
 Song, veiled in light like silver Artemis
  Shall yield to you.

34

" But all that's passed and over,
  And beggars mustn't choose,
For though our feet move proudly,
  There are holes within our shoes.

And though our hearts beat proudly,
  Yet have we lost the keys
Of all our golden gardens
  And Summer Palaces.

Oh, what's the use of gazing
  Back on the road behind,
When there's no friend or lover
  To bear your face in mind?

Once we were kings—what of it?
  The world forgets our name."

" *Yet must I still remember,*
  In secret, all the same? "

OH, will you not regret the shadows and the glooms,
The glowing fire at midnight in dark curtained rooms,
A step down which you stumbled in the dark unawares,
The ghost of mournful Beauty on the black oak stairs?

When all is tidied up and every corner clean,
Each window open wide, and nothing left unseen,
Even the skeleton removed from the little cupboard on
  the right,
And Silence, like a frightened bird, in headlong flight.

And where you walked, crushing dead leaves beneath
  your feet,
All now is hard—the asphalt pavement of a London
  street.
O, ancient woods which gossiped with the wind and rain !
New brooms sweep clean : these things, once gone, come
  not again !

FLAUNT not the splendour of thy beauty, June,
  On these weak eyes, unable to endure
Thy twilight, and thy morning, and thy noon,
  Lest, being blind with light, we find no cure.

Breathe not within our ears thy sultry song,
  Lest we forget and bear no more in mind
Our name, or the names of those we dwell among
  Because June's rapture leaves us deaf and blind.

Oh, blur thy roses in a mist of rain,
  Too fair, too fair for us, who still must go,
Solicitous and passionless and plain,
  Full of dull wisdom. Was it always so?

SHALL song despair
    That worthy praise
Is all too rare
    In these dull days?

The golden crown,
    The jewelled ring,
Rewards the clown,
    Evades the King.

Oh, there's no lack
    Of crowns at all
Bought from a Cheap Jack
    At a stall.

THE VISITOR

OH, when Joy comes, make no loud stir:
Let only silence welcome her!

Vagrant and shy, she perches on
Your heart a moment; then is gone

Like a bird behind a cloud.
O, eager heart, beat not so loud!

A RHYME

I'll blow a bubble
Of wet foam
And send my lover
A message home;
A splash of rain,
A glint of sea,
And that's the last
You'll hear of *me*!

ANOTHER RHYME

Oh, what had happened to the Moon,
She stared so crossly from the sky,
Glaring at all the passers-by,
As though she'd *bite* them very soon?
(Oh, *what* had happened to the Moon?)
Whilst a wind sang, with mouth awry,
Like an old organ out of tune.
Oh, what *had* happened to the Moon?
And nobody seemed scared but I.

QUATRAINS FROM "*A MASQUE OF EDINBURGH*"

MEN OF THE BRONZE AGE

OUR hands, but little different from the ape's,
    Did from unyielding granite and harsh stone
First fashion crude, grotesque yet human shapes,
    And left their signature on bronze and bone.

ROMANS

WE brought the straight road flung across the hills;
    Rule, rhythm and unswerving law we brought,
Which binds rebellious lust and riotous wills
    To the calm freedom of deliberate thought.

QUEEN MARGARET

I BROUGHT to Edinburgh law, music, peace,
    The first beginnings of the Art of Life,
Most difficult of all, and some release
    From petty bickering and mannerless strife.

ROBERT THE BRUCE

MINE the unshrinking sword: the floods poured down
    'Raging on Scotland; I the firmer stood,
And served this famous and disputed crown
    With great outpouring of heroic blood.

JAMES III

I LIT a bright, too-soon-extinguished flame;
    Craftsmen I loved and art, more than the sword.

COCHRANE

I BROUGHT the Scots the thistle and my fame,
    Then thrust my neck into a silken cord.

QUEEN MARY

I BROUGHT a gift of beauty. Who desire
    Beauty they understand not? Wherefore, I,
Having filled Scotland full of dangerous fire
    And bitter lovers, was condemned to die.

JOHN KNOX

I, FROM the ancient road our fathers trod,
    Austerely turned and tore apart the screen,
Set (as I deemed) betwixt Mankind and God,
    Obeyed my conscience and defied the Queen.

JAMES I

I LEFT my country for yon shining toun
    Ca'd London, and, like Solomon the Wise,
Who followed sin, found it not worth a croun :
    The thistle grows not well 'neath English skies.

COVENANTERS

WE set our heart and conscience, mind and will
    Against the King. Behold! Thy People stand
Jealous and watchful, flexible as steel,
    Lord, whilst thine enemies usurp thy land!

PRINCE CHARLIE

I BROUGHT to Scotland that enduring thing,
    Romantic memory, which shall prevail
When the renown of many a crownèd King,
    Conquest, reward, success and triumph fail.

BURNS

SCOTLAND I set to song. The poet dies :
    The song lives on. O, men of little wit,
Who see not with your own but through my eyes,
    Because I lived, but have small sense of it!